The Story of Jumping Mouse

LOTHROP, LEE & SHEPARD BOOKS · NEW YORK

A NATIVE AMERICAN LEGEND
RETOLD AND ILLUSTRATED BY

JOHN STEPTOE

The Story of

Jumping Mouse

LIBRARY OF CONGRESS CATALOGING IN PUBLICATION DATA

Steptoe, John, (date). The story of Jumping Mouse. Summary: The gifts of Magic Frog and his own hopeful and unselfish spirit bring Jumping Mouse finally to the Far-Off Land where no mouse goes hungry. 1. Indians of North America—Great Plains—Legends. [1. Indians of North America—Great Plains—Legends. 2. Mice—Fiction] I. Title. E78.G73S78 1983 398.2′08997 [E] 82-14848
ISBN 0-688-01902-1   ISBN 0-688-01903-X (lib. bdg.)

Design by Lynn Braswell

Once there was a young mouse who lived in the brush near a great river. During the day he and the other mice hunted for food. At night they gathered to hear the old ones tell stories. The young mouse liked to hear about the desert beyond the river, and he got shivers from the stories about the dangerous shadows that lived in the sky. But his favorite was the tale of the far-off land.

The far-off land sounded so wonderful the young mouse began to dream about it. He knew he would never be content until he had been there. The old ones warned that the journey would be long and perilous, but the young mouse would not be swayed. He set off one morning before the sun had risen.

It was evening before he reached the edge of the brush. Before him was the river; on the other side was the desert. The young mouse peered into the deep water. "How will I ever get across?" he said in dismay.

"Don't you know how to swim?" called a gravelly voice.

The young mouse looked around and saw a small green frog.

"Hello," he said. "What is swim?"

"This is swimming," said the frog, and she jumped into the river.

"Oh," said the young mouse, "I don't think I can do that."

"Why do you need to cross the river?" asked the frog, hopping back up the bank.

"I want to go to the far-off land," said the young mouse. "It sounds too beautiful to live a lifetime and not see it."

"In that case, you need my help. I'm Magic Frog. Who are you?"

"I'm a mouse," said the young mouse.

Magic Frog laughed. "That's not a name. I'll give you a name that will help you on your journey. I name you Jumping Mouse."

As soon as Magic Frog said this, the young mouse felt a strange tingling in his hind legs. He hopped a small hop and, to his surprise, jumped twice as high as he'd ever jumped before. "Thank you," he said, admiring his powerful new legs.

"You're welcome," said Magic Frog. "Now step onto this leaf and we'll cross the river together."

When they were safely on the other side, Magic Frog said, "You will encounter hardships on your way, but don't despair. You will reach the far-off land if you keep hope alive within you."

Jumping Mouse set off at once, hopping quickly from bush to bush. The shadows circled above, but he avoided being seen. He ate berries when he could find them and slept only when he was exhausted. Days passed. Though he was able to travel quickly, he began to wonder if he'd ever reach the other side of the desert. He then came upon a stream that coursed through the dry land. Under a large berry bush he met a fat old mouse.

"What strange hind legs you have," said the fat mouse.

"They were a gift from Magic Frog when she named me," said Jumping Mouse proudly.

"Humpf," snorted the fat mouse. "What good are they?"

"They've helped me come this far across the desert, and with luck they'll carry me to the far-off land," said Jumping Mouse. "But now I'm very tired. May I rest here a while?"

"Indeed you may," said the fat mouse. "In fact, you can stay forever."

"Thank you, but I'll stay only until I'm rested. I've seen the far-off land in my dreams and I must be on my way as soon as I'm able."

"Dreams," said the fat mouse scornfully. "I used to have such dreams, but all I ever found was desert. Why go jumping about the desert when everything anyone needs is right here?"

Jumping Mouse tried to explain that it wasn't a question of need, but something he felt he had to do. But the fat mouse only snorted again. Finally Jumping Mouse dug a hole and curled up for the night.

The next day the fat mouse warned him to stay on this side of the stream. "A snake lives on the other side," he said. "But don't worry. He's afraid of water, so he'll never cross the stream."

Life was easy beneath the berry bush, and Jumping Mouse was soon rested and strong. He and the fat mouse ate and slept and then slept and ate. Then one morning, when he went to the stream for a drink, he caught sight of his reflection. He was almost as fat as the fat old mouse!

"It's time for me to go on," thought Jumping Mouse. "I didn't come all this way to settle down under a berry bush."

Just then he noticed that a branch had gotten caught in the narrow of the stream. It spanned the water like a bridge—now the snake could cross! Jumping Mouse hurried back to warn the fat mouse. But the mousehole was empty, and there was a strange smell in the air. Snake. Jumping Mouse was too late. "Poor old friend," he thought as he hurried away. "He lost hope of finding his dream and now his life is over."

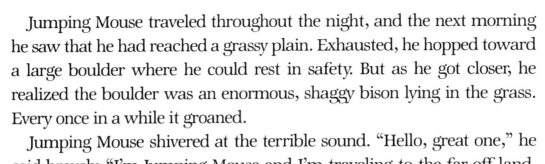

Jumping Mouse traveled throughout the night, and the next morning he saw that he had reached a grassy plain. Exhausted, he hopped toward a large boulder where he could rest in safety. But as he got closer, he realized the boulder was an enormous, shaggy bison lying in the grass. Every once in a while it groaned.

Jumping Mouse shivered at the terrible sound. "Hello, great one," he said bravely. "I'm Jumping Mouse and I'm traveling to the far-off land. Why do you lie here as if you were dying?"

"Because I *am* dying," said the bison. "I drank from a poisoned stream, and it blinded me. I can't see to find tender grass to eat or sweet water to drink. I'll surely die."

Jumping Mouse was sad to see so wondrous a beast so helpless. "When I began my journey," he said, "Magic Frog gave me a name and strong legs to carry me to the far-off land. My magic is not as powerful as hers, but I'll do what I can to help you. I name you Eyes-of-a-Mouse."

As soon as he had spoken Jumping Mouse heard the bison snort with joy. He heard but he could no longer see, for he had given the bison his own sight.

"Thank you," said Eyes-of-a-Mouse. "You are small, but you have done a great thing. If you will hop along beneath me, the shadows of the sky won't see you, and I will guide you to the mountains."

Jumping Mouse did as he was told. He hopped to the rhythm of the bison's hooves, and in this way he reached the foot of the mountains.

"I am an animal of the plains, so I must stop here," said Eyes-of-a-Mouse. "How will you cross the mountains when you can't see?"

"There will be a way," said Jumping Mouse. "Hope is alive within me." He said good-bye to his friend; then he dug a hole and went to sleep.

The next morning Jumping Mouse woke to cool breezes that blew down from the mountain peaks. Cautiously he set out in the direction of the coolness. He had not gone far when he felt fur beneath his paws. He jumped back in alarm and sniffed the air. Wolf! He froze in terror, but when nothing happened he gathered up his courage and said, "Excuse me. I'm Jumping Mouse, and I'm traveling to the far-off land. Can you tell me the way?"

"I would if I could," said the wolf, "but a wolf finds his way with his nose, and mine will no longer smell for me."

"What happened?" asked Jumping Mouse.

"I was once a proud and lazy creature," replied the wolf. "I misused the gift of smell, and so I lost it. I have learned not to be proud, but without my nose to tell me where I am and where I am going, I cannot survive. I am lying here waiting for the end."

Jumping Mouse was saddened by the wolf's story. He told him about Magic Frog and Eyes-of-a-Mouse. "I have a little magic left," he said. "I'll be happy to help you. I name you Nose-of-a-Mouse."

The wolf howled for joy. Jumping Mouse could hear him sniffing the air, taking in the mountain fragrances. But Jumping Mouse could no longer smell the pine-scented breezes. He no longer had the use of his nose or his eyes. "You are but a small creature," said Nose-of-a-Mouse, "but you have given me a great gift. You must let me thank you. Come, hop along beneath where the shadows of the sky won't see you. I will guide you through the mountains to the far-off land."

So Jumping Mouse hopped to the rhythm of the wolf's padding paws, and in this way he reached the far-off land.

"I am an animal of the mountains, so I must stop here," said Nose-of-a-Mouse. "How will you manage if you can no longer see or smell?"

"There will be a way," said Jumping Mouse. He then said good-bye to his friend and dug a hole and went to sleep.

The next morning Jumping Mouse woke up and crawled from his hole. "I am here," he said. "I feel the earth beneath my paws. I hear the wind rustling leaves on the trees. The sun warms my bones. All is not lost, but I'll never be as I was. How will I ever manage?" Then Jumping Mouse began to cry.

"Jumping Mouse," he heard a gravelly voice say.

"Magic Frog, is that you?" Jumping Mouse asked, swallowing his tears.

"Yes," said Magic Frog. "Don't cry, Jumping Mouse. Your unselfish spirit has brought you great hardship, but it is that same spirit of hope and compassion that has brought you to the far-off land."

"You have nothing to fear, Jumping Mouse."

"Jump high, Jumping Mouse," commanded Magic Frog.

Jumping Mouse did as he was told and jumped as high as he could. Then he felt the air lifting him higher still into the sky. He stretched out his paws in the sun and felt strangely powerful. To his joy he began to see the wondrous beauty of the world above and below and to smell the scent of earth and sky and living things.

"Jumping Mouse," he heard Magic Frog call. "I give you a new name."

"You are now called Eagle,

and you will live in the far-off land forever."